This Book is a Gift from
Bring Me A Book™ Foundation

CONSEJOS PARA LEER EN VOZ ALTA

- Deje que su niño escoja el libro
- ¡Acurrúquense juntos!
- Lea despacio
- Lea el título del libro y el nombre del autor
- Deje que su niño voltee las páginas
- Haga predicciones
- Motive y elogie a su hijo
- ¡Sea juguetón, dramático, y i Diviértanse!

MISS MAGGIE

ALSO BY CYNTHIA RYLANT

When I Was Young in the Mountains

MISS MAGGIE

by Cynthia Rylant

illustrated by Thomas Di Grazia

DUTTON CHILDREN'S BOOKS   NEW YORK

Library of Congress Cataloging in Publication Data

Rylant, Cynthia.   Miss Maggie.

Summary: Young Nat is afraid of old Miss Maggie and her
rotting log house until his heart conquers his fears.
[1. Old age—Fiction]   I. Di Grazia, Thomas, ill.
II. Title
PZ7.R982Mi   1983   [E]   82-18206
ISBN 0-525-44048-8

Published in the United States by
Dutton Children's Books,
a division of Penguin Books USA Inc.
375 Hudson Street
New York, New York 10014

Editor: Ann Durell   Designer: Claire Counihan

Printed in U.S.A.   First Edition
15 14 13 12 11 10 9 8

for Nathaniel and his Nana
C. R.

for Phyllis
T. D. G.

Maggie Ziegler lived in a rotting log house on the edge of Crawford's pasture. There was always a nosy old cow peering in one of her windows. And some folks said a black snake hung from the rafters inside and that it ate all the mice that hid in the cupboards.

While a Guernsey peered in a window on one side of the house, Nat Crawford sometimes had his nose mashed up against a window on the opposite side. He was always looking for that snake. What he finally found is a story worth telling.

Nat had been only as far as Maggie Ziegler's front porch. That's where he'd stand with a gallon of buttermilk or a kettle of beans that his grandmother sent over to Miss Maggie. With his arms full, Nat would knock his toe against the bottom of the old screen door, and pretty soon Miss Maggie would stick her head out.

She'd let out a little snort and smack her lips and say, "Well, well. Come right in, come right in here, boy."

But Nat never did. He'd mumble something or other, take a quick peek at her rafters, and setting the jug or the kettle at her feet, he'd turn and run for all he was worth, across the fields toward home. He wouldn't look back until he was safely on his side of the barbed wire. Then he'd give a little kick, because he still hadn't got a glimpse of that snake.

Miss Maggie tended a garden alongside the old log house. But what with cows, dogs, and boys occasionally passing through, Miss Maggie's garden didn't grow a lot. Still, there was always a potato or two to boil. Nat would see Miss Maggie rising up from the soil, her brown, wrinkled face partly hidden by a faded blue bonnet, and he'd watch while she shuffled back to the house with an apron filled with a few vegetables that had survived.

Sometimes Miss Maggie rode to the grocery store with Nat and his grandfather. Nat would wait in the truck when Miss Maggie went into the store, because she always had a wad of tobacco in her jaw and she'd spit it just anywhere she pleased. Nat was afraid people might think she was a relative.

Nat didn't see much of Miss Maggie in the winter. Everybody in the country holed up—with lots of canned goods for the pantry, and wood and coal for the fires—to wait out the snow. But there was always a ribbon of smoke rising up from Miss Maggie's chimney in the mornings, and Nat knew that she and the snake were making it okay.

But one morning as Nat went out to feed the guinea
hens, he noticed that Miss Maggie's chimney wasn't
puffing a bit. It just stood cold and hard, atop the
rotting house. Nat set down the bucket of feed and
wriggled between the barbed wire. His boots made
loud crunching sounds as he ran across the frozen field.

Careful to avoid the tricky board that rocked when he stepped on it, Nat walked across the snowy porch and knocked (with his hand, this time) on the old screen door.

Nothing.

No lip-smacking, wrinkled old head stuck out the door.

Just nothing.

Nat ran around to the side of the house, but the windows were all frosted over.

He ran back to the porch. He looked across the snow and wondered about getting Grandad.

No.

He took a deep breath and pulled back the screen door. He put a stiff, gloved hand on the knob.

The door opened.

Nat tried to call out, but his throat froze up on him. It was hard to see anything, dark as it was in the icy room. Nat propped back the door to let some light in.

There she was.

Miss Maggie was sitting huddled in a corner, next to the empty fireplace. Her head hung forward limply, and she clutched a bundle of cloth in her hands.

If his feet had listened to his head, Nat would have bounded out of that house in a flash. But his feet weren't listening. Only his heart.

"Miss Maggie?" Nat waited for the old head to move. It didn't.

He took a few steps.

"Miss Maggie?"

The head moved slightly. Or did he imagine it?
He walked over and squatted down beside her.

"Miss Maggie? You sick?"

The old woman slowly raised her head. Her eyes
were lost in bags of wrinkled flesh, and their rims
looked red.

"Henry," she whispered.

"No, it's me. Nat."

She held up the bundle of cloth.

"Henry."

Nat took the bundle from her. He was sure the snake must have died on her. But wrapped in the rags wasn't a snake. It was a starling.

Miss Maggie's shoulders trembled.

"My Henry," she whispered again.

Nat looked at the dead bird, its feathers all matted and frozen. Then he wrapped it up carefully.

"C'mon, Miss Maggie." Nat took her bony hand. "My Grandad will know what to do."

They walked across the field hand in hand, the boy balancing dead Henry under one arm, the old woman gripping a tattered quilt about her shoulders. They had to take the long way around the road, as Nat wasn't sure Miss Maggie could squeeze through the fence.

Nat saw a lot of Miss Maggie that winter, and for many winters after. She saved all her tobacco tins for him, so he might have a special place to put shiny pebbles and fat bugs. And he decorated coffee cans with foil and leaves and ribbons, so she might have a proper place to spit.

He also found out that a black snake never lived in her house, after all. So—

One day in the spring, he brought her one—
and its name was Henry.